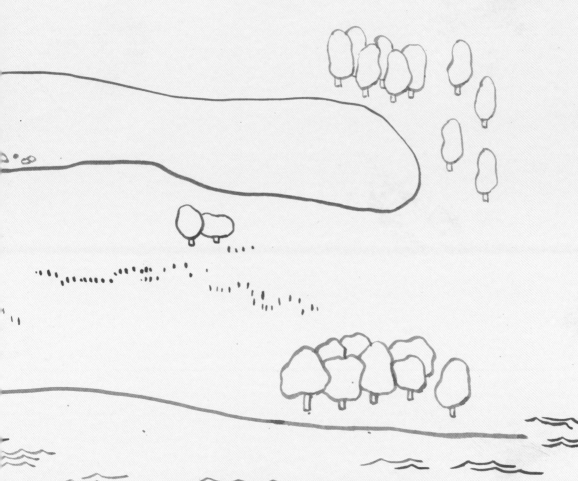

For Katie, Max, and Holt.
And to the path along the
river that I walked every
day during this past year.

—Reif

The Path
A Story About Finding Your Way

Written by Reif Larsen
Illustrated by Marine Schneider

This book was conceived, edited,
and designed by Little Gestalten

Edited by Robert Klanten and
Maria-Elisabeth Niebius

Typeface: Rooney by Jan Fromm

Printed by Schleunungdruck GmbH
Made in Germany

Published by Little Gestalten,
Berlin, 2021

ISBN 978-3-96704-707-3

© Die Gestalten Verlag GmbH & Co. KG, Berlin, 2021

For more information, and to order books, please visit
www.little.gestalten.com.

Bibliographic information published by the Deutsche
Nationalbibliothek. The Deutsche Nationalbibliothek
lists this publication in the Deutsche Nationalbibliografie;
detailed bibliographic data are available online at
www.dnb.de

MIX
Paper from
responsible sources
FSC® C105039

This book was printed on
paper certified according
to the standards of the FSC®.

The Path

A Story About Finding Your Way

Written by Reif Larsen
Illustrated by Marine Schneider

LITTLE
GESTALTEN

If you know where to look, you will find a path on the edge of a small city. The path winds its way through woods until it reaches a river.

Every year, the path changes a little.
Now, it's early spring. Everywhere you
look, there are tiny, electric-green buds.

People walk their dogs on the path.
People come to watch the birds. People
come to the path when they are sad.
Or happy. Or somewhere in between.

Luca comes to the path after school. Luca has discovered a civilization of alien twig creatures. He calls them *Tontos*. They live in towers covered with eyes, keeping watch on the path.

Clara is a scientist. Clara keeps a little notebook and a magnifying glass with her at all times.

Clara loves to look at the smallest of things: ants, beetles, water droplets, the pollen of a flower.

Her mother tells Clara to watch where she is going. But Clara is watching. All the time.

A dung beetle, Anoplotrupes stercorosus

Clara and Luca sometimes run into each other on the path, but Luca's path is not Clara's path.

Luca's aliens and Clara's ants don't speak the same language yet.

In the evening, the woods settle down. A fox emerges from his den. For him, the path is home.

The next day, Avi appears, walking his dog, Moo.

Moo has more energy than one dog should have. He leaps and gallops around while Avi listens to the thump of drums on his headphones.

Moo can smell the
fox and makes little
whining noises.

"Come on," says Avi.
"Let's get out of here."

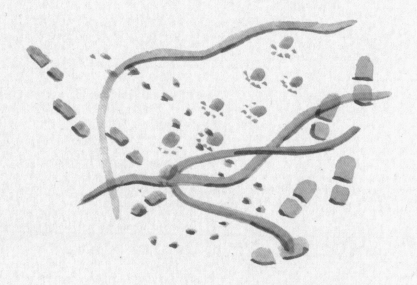

The rain comes. Plants begin to grow. The path becomes muddy.

Prints appear—boots, paws, feet, hands, bicycle tracks.

One day Luca finds Clara
hunched over, looking.

Luca works up his courage.
"Watcha you doing?"

"He's wounded," Clara says.

"Who?" Luca asks.

"A red fox," Clara says. "*Vulpes
vulpes.* It's his back right foot."

Clara points. "Normally, a fox
will step into his own footprints
with each step. Not him."

Clara teaches Luca how to read footprints. Toes and pads and hooves are like words in a book. Luca's aliens are curious too. They help Luca and Clara look for clues.

Clara and Luca hear footsteps. Avi and Moo are barreling down the path.

"Watch out!" Avi says.

They let Avi and Moo by. The forest grows quiet again. They keep exploring. They are making a book of path prints.

"Tomorrow?" Luca asks.

"Tomorrow," Clara says.

That night, the red fox,
Vulpes vulpes, sniffs
the ground, reading the
day's stories. He limps
off into the brush,
searching for dinner.

The next day, Luca and Clara
come back with a fried egg.

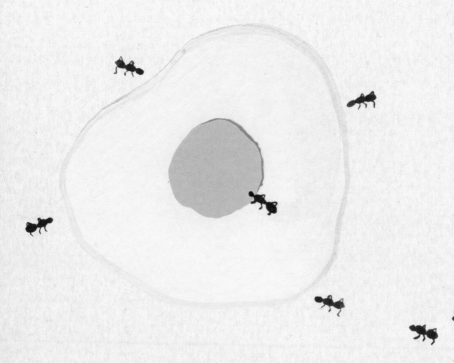

"Do foxes like eggs?"
asks Luca.

"I think so," says Clara.
"Don't you?"

"Yes," says Luca.
"But I'm not a fox."

"Maybe you are," says Clara.

Luca's eyes go wide. Luca stares
at his hands for a long time,
wondering what it feels like
to have paws.

Later, Avi and Moo come crashing through. Avi's headphones get caught on a branch. The music stops.

Moo goes stiff. Avi looks out into the forest.

A fox!

The fox turns and limps away.

Avi listens. Birdsong. The rustle of leaves. The sound of his own heartbeat.

That night, the sky is clear. Three deer step onto the path. They follow the trail, then step off again.

On the first hot day of the year,
the woods grow full with life.
Insects dance, snakes wriggle,
birds collect strange objects
to build their nests.

Clara and Luca have made an observation post. Clara is teaching Luca about how ants make trails using scents. Luca is showing Clara how the *Tontos* hide their treasures inside the trees.

Clara and Luca look up. Avi is staring
into the woods. Moo isn't with him.

"Have you seen the fox?" Avi asks.

Clara blinks. Nods. "He got better."

"How do you know?" Avi says.

"The path," says Clara.